GIRLS SURVIVE

Girls Survive is published by Stone Arch Books
A Capstone Imprint
1710 Roe Crest Drive
North Mankato, Minnesota 56003
www.capstonepub.com

Library of Congress Cataloging-in-Publication Data
Names: Smith, Nikki Shannon, 1971– author. | Trunfio, Alessia, 1990– illustrator.
Title: Charlotte spies for justice : a Civil War survival story / by Nikki Shannon Smith ; illustrated by Alessia Trunfio.
Other titles: Girls survive.
Description: North Mankato, Minnesota : an imprint of Stone Arch Books, [2019] | Series: Girls survive | Summary: In 1864, twelve-year-old former slave Charlotte is lucky enough to live on a plantation near Richmond, Virginia, owned by a Miss Van Lew, who hates slavery. When Charlotte overhears a conversation, she realizes that her mistress is gathering information and passing it on to the Union army. Charlotte is eager to help, (especially since her own cousin, Mary, is involved) but her enthusiasm may endanger them all—or help free 400 Union soldiers who are being moved from Richmond farther south.
Identifiers: LCCN 2019000274| ISBN 9781496583840 (hardcover) | ISBN 9781496584465 (pbk.) | ISBN 9781496583895 (ebook pdf)
Subjects: LCSH: African American girls—Juvenile fiction. | Cousins—Juvenile fiction. | Women spies—Juvenile fiction. | Slavery—United States—Juvenile fiction. | Adventure stories. | Virginia—History—Civil War, 1861-1865—Juvenile fiction. | Confederate States of America—History—Juvenile fiction. | United States—History—Civil War, 1861-1865—Juvenile fiction. | CYAC: African Americans—Fiction. | Cousins—Fiction. | Spies—Fiction. | Slavery—Fiction. | Confederate States of America—Fiction. | Adventure and adventurers—Fiction. | Virginia—History—Civil War, 1861-1865—Fiction. | United States—History—Civil War, 1861-1865—Fiction. | LCGFT: Historical fiction. | Action and adventure fiction. | Spy fiction.
Classification: LCC PZ7.S6566 Ch 2019 | DDC 813.6 [Fic]—dc23
LC record available at https://lccn.loc.gov/2019000274

Designer:
Charmaine Whitman

Image credits:
AFBPhotography: Alan Bradley, 112; Alamy: Virginia Museum of History & Culture, 107; Shutterstock: kaokiemonkey (pattern), back cover and throughout, Max Lashcheuski (background), 2 and throughout

CHAPTER ONE

Richmond, Virginia
Miss Van Lew's home
January 29, 1864

A lot of people came and went from Miss Van Lew's big old house at the top of Church Hill. It was hard to know who they were. Some were white, and some were colored. Some I never saw again, and a few seemed to be Miss Van Lew's friends. All I knew was that my favorite was Mister McNiven. He owned the town bakery and visited us every single day.

Most of Miss Van Lew's visitors didn't pay any mind to a twelve-year-old colored girl, but Mister

McNiven did. Besides Miss Van Lew, he was the nicest white person I'd ever met. He always said, "Mornin', Charlotte. It's a good day to be alive." Then he'd hand me a whole loaf of fresh bread, just for me.

I don't know why Mister McNiven always said it was a good day to be alive. The North and the South had been at war for three long years now. Every day was full of battles and dead soldiers and hoping the North would win. Even though I lived in the South, where slavery was alive and well, I knew the North was right. I had been a slave, and it was horrible.

Miss Van Lew hated slavery too. One time she'd said, "It just makes me sick to see one human being act as if it's OK to own another."

Her daddy used to have slaves right on this very farm. He'd died before I was even born, and Miss Van Lew had freed all his slaves. She'd wanted to right his wrong. My cousin Mary had been one of those slaves. After she'd freed her, Miss Van Lew had even sent Mary to the North to go to school for a while.

That had all happened while I was a slave on a plantation in Maryland. But Miss Van Lew had been so mad at her daddy that she'd looked for the kin of all his slaves and freed them too. She'd found me four years ago and bought my freedom. She even gave me a place to live and work at Church Hill. She never did find my mama and daddy, though.

My cousin Mary was the only family I had. The first time we met, we'd hugged like we'd known each other all our lives. "You're in good hands now," Mary had said. "I'll take care of you."

And that's just what she did. Mary and I were like two peas in a pod, and she treated me like her little sister. We'd shared a cabin across from the main house for a year. Mary used to borrow books from Miss Van Lew to read to me. Sometimes we'd stayed up late, and Mary had taught me to read by the light of the fire. But now she worked somewhere else—I wasn't sure where—and I never got to see her.

I missed Mary every day, but I was still glad to be where I was. Every morning I stood on Miss Van Lew's porch and waited for Mister McNiven, and today was no different. I wrapped my old blanket tightly around my shoulders and shivered as I watched for the bakery wagon. It felt as if the cold was trying to bite me.

My mind wandered while I waited, and I thought of Mister McNiven's words. *Maybe it's a good day to be alive because there is still hope,* I thought. *Maybe the North will win the war.* It was time for slavery to end, so I kept my fingers crossed for the Union soldiers.

"Charlotte? There's still no sign of Thomas McNiven?" Miss Van Lew's voice drifted down the stairs and right out to the porch.

"No, Miss Van Lew!" I called back. Mister McNiven did seem to be a little bit later than usual, but I didn't see any reason to worry. Miss Van Lew sounded concerned, though.

From outside I could hear her upstairs, making all kinds of bumps and thumps. She was always moving furniture around up there. Truth be told, Miss Van Lew was odd. First off, she was a white lady in the South who didn't like slavery. Second, even though my job was to keep the house clean, I wasn't even allowed to go in half the rooms.

Miss Van Lew had told me a couple of years back that I was to stay out of any room with a closed door. Even though I thought it was odd, I listened for two reasons: I knew what happened to colored people who broke the rules, and I was grateful to Miss Van Lew for getting me out of where I'd been.

The other thing was, Miss Van Lew kept strange company. Some of the slaves she freed stayed on, and they were in and out of the house like family. Sometimes she took them up to one of her private rooms to talk. Confederates—the southerners fighting against the Union—stopped by sometimes too. I don't know why Miss Van Lew was friends with them, since they were fighting to keep slavery, but she was.

Miss Van Lew didn't know it, but I'd also seen Union soldiers visit her at night. It had only happened once—at least that I knew of. I'd been checking on my little flower garden, just outside my cabin, when they came. But by the time I'd woken up the next morning and gotten to the main house, the soldiers were gone.

Even though I'd been curious about it, I'd never said anything. I probably wasn't supposed to have seen them, and I didn't want Miss Van Lew mad at me. Odd or not, I liked her.

Just then Miss Van Lew shouted again: "You still don't see him?"

Now *I* was getting a little bit concerned—and hungry. I always ate Mister McNiven's bread as soon as he gave it to me, and my stomach was growling. Just when I was about to shout back to say I still didn't see him, there he was, coming slowly up the steep hill in his wagon.

I spotted him right away. You could see just about all of Richmond from Miss Van Lew's house.

"Here he comes!" I yelled back over my shoulder.

The wagon pulled up, and Mister McNiven stomped up the white cement stairs in his big,

heavy boots. He didn't have any bread in his hands, and his mouth was turned down like I'd never seen it before.

"Mornin', Charlotte," he said.

I smiled. "Mornin', Mister McNiven."

Mister McNiven didn't smile back. And he didn't say, "It's a good day to be alive." He just headed straight for the front door.

I opened it for him, and by the time we both got inside, Miss Van Lew was already on her way downstairs. Her smile disappeared as soon as she got a good look at Mister McNiven's face.

"Let's go on upstairs, Thomas," she said.

And that was it. Up they went, leaving me standing alone downstairs with nothing but my empty stomach.

If Miss Van Lew had company upstairs, I was supposed to wait in the kitchen until they left, so I went to wash the breakfast dishes. But

Mister McNiven's face wouldn't leave my mind. Something was wrong—very wrong. I owed it to Mister McNiven to see if I could help.

Even though I knew I wasn't supposed to, I went up the stairs and tiptoed down the hall until I could hear voices behind one of the closed doors. Then I squatted down next to the little table of cupid statues Miss Van Lew loved so much and put my ear close to the door. I could barely hear what they were saying.

As far as I knew, Miss Van Lew and Mister McNiven were alone, but they whispered anyway. It just didn't make any sense. Then I heard something that made my breath catch.

"Are you sure that's what Mary said?" asked Miss Van Lew.

Mary. Were they talking about *my* Mary? I closed my eyes and focused so I could hear better.

"I'm positive," Mister McNiven said, raising his voice a bit. "I delivered bread to the Confederate

White House this morning as usual. Mary met me outside like always, but this time I could see on her face that she had something big to tell me."

"Tell me again," said Miss Van Lew.

"The Confederates are moving the Union prisoners south," Mister McNiven whispered. "Mary said she heard them talking about it at dinner last night."

Miss Van Lew's voice was quiet but very matter-of-fact. "This type of information is exactly why I placed Mary in the Confederate White House," she said. "It's invaluable to the Union. We'll have to get the message to General Butler right away."

I couldn't believe my own ears. Miss Van Lew had sent my cousin Mary to the Confederates? Mary knew Confederate secrets and was passing them to Miss Van Lew? And Miss Van Lew was passing them to the Union? That could only mean one thing—they were all spies!

I leaned back to let that sink into my mind for a minute. But as I did, I bumped into the table of cupids. One crashed to the floor and shattered into a hundred pieces. I froze.

CHAPTER TWO

Richmond, Virginia
Miss Van Lew's home
January 29, 1864

"Somebody is outside that door," I heard Miss Van Lew say. Her footsteps got closer and closer.

There was no way I could run down the hall fast enough. I knelt down, tucked my head, and covered my face with my hands as the lock clicked.

A moment later, the door opened, and I could see the tips of Miss Van Lew's boots right in front of my knees.

"Get up, Charlotte," she said.

I stood up but kept my eyes on the floor. All zmy muscles were tight. I hadn't been hit since I was free, but I'd never given Miss Van Lew any reason to be mad at me before.

"Look at me," Miss Van Lew said.

I kept my chin down and put my eyes up. Mister McNiven was in the doorway watching us.

Miss Van Lew's eyebrows were so frowned up they were almost touching. "Charlotte, were you eavesdropping?"

"Yes, ma'am," I said.

"What did you hear?" Miss Van Lew asked. Her hands stayed at her sides, so I figured she wasn't going to hit me.

I lifted my chin, took a deep breath, and got the truth ready to come out. "I heard that Mary sent you a message," I said. "That Union soldiers are being moved from the prison. They're being taken south."

Miss Van Lew glanced at Mister McNiven, then looked at me again. "That's all?"

"No, ma'am," I said. "I heard you say you were going to tell the Union about it."

Miss Van Lew was quiet for a long time. I had no idea what she was going to say to me, but I knew what I wanted to say to her. I wanted to ask if I could be a spy too. I wanted to help the Union win the war and end slavery.

Finally Miss Van Lew said, "You have no idea how dangerous this is, Charlotte. If the Confederates find out Mary is giving us information, everything will be ruined. If we get caught, they'll kill Mary."

A single tear made its way down my cheek. The idea of losing Mary was more than I could take.

"Miss Elizabeth," said Mister McNiven, "don't be too hard on her. She's just a girl."

Miss Van Lew stared at him. "She's a girl who might get us all killed."

"I won't tell," I said. "I promise."

"Who would she tell anyway?" asked Mister McNiven.

Miss Van Lew marched past Mister McNiven and went back into the secret room. "Come in here and shut the door, Charlotte," she said sternly.

I did as I was told. I'd never been in this room before, and it wasn't like the ones I'd cleaned. There were blankets nailed up over the windows, and the only light was from a lantern in the corner. There was a big pile of blankets and sheets, but no bed. There was also a table with all kinds of little bottles that looked like medicine. There was a black bag on the table too, the kind doctors carried.

Mister McNiven and Miss Van Lew sat down in the only two chairs. I stood there clutching my blanket around my shoulders.

"I don't know what to do with you, Charlotte," said Miss Van Lew.

"I won't tell anyone," I said. "I'm glad you're helping the Union."

Mister McNiven chuckled. "See there, she won't tell."

"People make mistakes," said Miss Van Lew. "If she's ever questioned, they'll do whatever they have to do to get answers out of her."

"Miss Van Lew, I'd die before I told anyone." I meant it. I took a deep breath and looked her in the eyes. "I want to be a spy too."

Miss Van Lew's thin lips got so thin they disappeared. "I am *not* a spy," she said. "I am a patriot. I want to see my country united and *all* people free."

I blinked. It sounded like she thought *spy* was a bad word, but I didn't think that at all. It was brave and heroic . . . and right.

Mister McNiven watched us with a curious look on his face. He must have gotten tired of the quiet, because eventually he said, "Charlotte might be helpful to us, Miss Elizabeth. Nobody would suspect her."

Miss Van Lew was as still as a statue. Finally she said, "She *is* smart, just like her cousin."

I smiled proudly. "Miss Van Lew, I know I can do it."

"You might be right," she said. "But are you really willing to risk your life?"

I took a deep breath. "Yes, ma'am. Now that my life is my own, I'm willing to give it away if it helps free my people," I said.

"Very well," said Miss Van Lew. "Since you know what we're doing, you might as well help. You're in danger either way. You will be my assistant. Your first mission will be tomorrow."

I smiled again and exhaled.

"Don't smile," she said. "You're going to be visiting the most horrible place you've ever been."

I doubted that, but I didn't argue. I'd already been someplace horrible. I'd seen hate so deep people wore it on their faces. I'd seen death. I'd seen slavery.

"Tomorrow," Miss Van Lew continued, "you'll accompany me to Libby Prison to deliver a message." Her voice got so low I had to lean toward her to hear. "The prison is full of Union soldiers who were caught by the Confederates. Most are injured or ill—or both. They're starving and lonely."

"Is that where you go every week?" I asked. At least once a week I had noticed Miss Van Lew loading a basket into her wagon, but I never knew where she was headed.

Miss Van Lew nodded. "I've been going since it opened. I started out taking food and medicine and books to the prisoners. Eventually I realized I could gain information from the soldiers, and even some of the guards."

I was quiet as she spoke. Miss Van Lew had friends I hadn't known she had, but as I would soon learn, she also had enemies.

"Charlotte, you listen to me and listen good," she continued. "A lot of people don't like that I show sympathy toward the Union soldiers. I think some might even be suspicious. They will like you even less."

That didn't worry me at all. A lot of white southerners didn't like colored people. I had learned to not let people's dislike for me upset me. But what Miss Van Lew said next did.

"Some of these people will want to kill you, just because of the color of your skin," she told me. "And if you get caught helping the Union, they won't just kill you. They will whip you first.

And they'll come for Mary. Her fate will be the same."

I swallowed the lump in my throat. "Yes, ma'am," I said.

It didn't matter if I was afraid. All that mattered was getting the work done without getting caught— and that was what I'd do.

CHAPTER THREE

Richmond, Virginia
Miss Van Lew's home
January 30, 1864

Miss Van Lew and I stayed up all night getting ready for the trip to Libby Prison. I sat at the kitchen table and watched her place items in a basket. She put in some normal things, like bread and milk and medicine.

But that wasn't all. She spent most of the night hiding a message in a book. She underlined words and poked holes.

When I asked her what it meant, she just said, "The prisoners will know." Then she tucked the book in the basket.

While Miss Van Lew worked, she gave me some rules to follow. "Act like a slave, not an employee," she said. "You have to look like you're afraid of everyone."

"Yes, Miss Van Lew," I said. That part would be easy.

Next she said, "Be as unnoticeable as you can. Don't speak unless you're asked a direct question, and answer with your eyes down. Getting noticed will cause a problem."

I knew Miss Van Lew was trying to keep me safe, but these things were obvious. I'd spent most of my life doing them anyway. If she'd said, "Act like a slave," that would have been enough.

There was one thing on my mind, though. Finally I gathered up my courage and asked the question that had been pestering me all night. "Miss Van Lew, why did you send Mary to the Confederate White House?"

Miss Van Lew put down the socks she was folding and stared at me. "The Confederate White House," she said, "is full of useful information. It's also full of ignorant people who will assume that, as a colored woman, Mary can't read. I knew they'd be careless around her. Plus, her memory is flawless." Then she picked up the socks again.

It all made perfect sense. Mary could read their papers and eavesdrop without them suspecting her. "She must know all kinds of secrets," I said.

Miss Van Lew didn't say anything. She put several pairs of socks in the basket. Then she put gingerbread and a bottle of buttermilk on top. "It's time to go," she said.

I was surprised Miss Van Lew didn't change into nicer clothes, but I wrapped up in my blanket and followed her outside. The sun was just coming up and warmed the air a bit.

We climbed into the wagon and headed down the hill. The bouncing of the wagon shook up my stomach, which was already sick with nerves. The closer we got to Libby Prison, the worse I felt. By the time the wagon stopped, though, I had calmed myself down. I was ready to do my job.

Richmond, Virginia
Libby Prison

I climbed down from the wagon and stared up at the three-story brick building in front of me. Even from the outside, Libby Prison looked miserable. The windows were just openings in the walls with no glass. I knew from living in the cabins on the plantation how cold it must be inside.

From a second-floor window a thin, pale face stared down at me. I knew I was looking at the face of a Union soldier—a man who risked his life to fight for my freedom. Now he was a captive, just as I had been before Miss Van Lew freed me. It made me want the Confederates to lose even more.

A guard walked toward us, and Miss Van Lew said, "Don't just stand there, Charlotte, get the basket."

I hurried and did what she said, sneaking a look at the man who'd approached us. He smiled at Miss Van Lew, but something about him was as cold as a January night.

"I brought your favorites," said Miss Van Lew. "Gingerbread and buttermilk." She motioned for me to get the gift out of the basket, so I did. I kept my eyes down and my mouth shut, just like I had when I was a slave.

"Well, that's mighty kind, Miss Elizabeth," said the guard. His voice sounded as if he had rocks in his throat. "Who's this little thing with you?"

My heartbeat sped up. The last thing I wanted was this guard's attention on me before we even got inside. I could feel him looking at me, but I didn't look up.

Miss Van Lew said, "This is my servant girl. She'll be helping me today. You'll have to excuse us. I'm not feeling very well. I'm going to deliver these gifts and go on home."

Miss Van Lew hurried inside the prison, and I hurried right along with her, making sure to stand behind her the whole way. We went up some stairs to the second floor. The room wasn't quite as cold as I thought it would be—there were bodies everywhere, warming it up. It smelled like decay and sweat.

My heart broke when I saw the Union soldiers. There were so many of them. Some sat or lay down on the cold wooden floor. The man who'd been looking out the window when we arrived was

still standing there, but he'd turned around to look at me. His cheeks were sunken in, which made his eyes look very large. His shirt was stained with blood.

My sadness switched to anger. The Confederates didn't care about anyone but their own greedy selves. All they cared about was money, owning slaves, and getting their way. I was so caught up in what I saw, I almost let Miss Van Lew walk to the back of the room without me.

I followed her to a man reading a book. He looked up and smiled at her. Even though I kept my eyes down, I noticed a guard at the door staring at us.

Miss Van Lew said, "Good Morning, Charles. How are you feeling today?"

"Better," Charles said. He handed her the book he'd been reading. "Thank you for letting me borrow your book."

"You're welcome," Miss Van Lew replied. "Would you like another?"

Charles nodded. Miss Van Lew reached into the basket and gave him the book she'd put in there last night—the one with the message in it. Then she turned to me.

"Give him a piece of bread, Charlotte," she said. "A little milk too."

I followed Miss Van Lew as she made her way around the room. We gave small pieces of bread and sips of milk to some of the Union soldiers. Miss Van Lew gave medicine to a few other men. She also gave socks to several soldiers—the man at the window, a man shivering against the cold, stone wall, and a few men who had nothing on their feet at all.

The whole time, I felt the guard's eyes on us. It was as if he was trying to burn holes through our skin.

Miss Van Lew and I didn't say a single word all the way home. As soon as we climbed out of the wagon, I went straight into the kitchen and prepared Miss Van Lew's lunch. She went upstairs to put on a fresh dress.

I had just set lunch out on the kitchen table when someone banged on the front door. I ran to answer it. Miss Van Lew was right behind me. A colored man I'd seen coming and going many times stood on the porch. He never seemed to stay for long.

Miss Van Lew spoke from behind me. "Good afternoon, Abraham."

"Miss Van Lew," the man said, "you've got company coming." He paused as if he was waiting for something.

"You can go ahead and speak in front of Charlotte," Miss Van Lew said. "She's working with us now."

I felt ten feet tall when she said that. Abraham grinned at me and said, "One of the guards is suspicious. He didn't like that you brought a colored girl to the prison. I guess it was Charlotte?"

Miss Van Lew said, "Yes, it was. And I don't care if he liked it or not."

"Well, I heard he's coming tonight to take your horse," said Abraham. "Claims the Confederates need more of them for the men. You'd better make sure you're ready."

"Oh, I'll be ready," Miss Van Lew said, looking determined. She handed Abraham a pair of boots. Without another word, he turned around and walked down the steps.

The whole thing was a bit strange to me, but like I said, Miss Van Lew was odd.

When we were alone again, Miss Van Lew turned to me. "We've got a job to do, Charlotte," she said. "They're not getting my horse. They're not getting my secrets. And they're not getting us."

CHAPTER FOUR

Richmond, Virginia
Miss Van Lew's home
January 30, 1864

Miss Van Lew shut the front door and turned to me. "We've got to hurry, Charlotte," she said. "Clear the table from this morning and hide those eggs. Pull all the curtains shut."

"Yes, Miss Van Lew," I said, nodding.

"Cut up some carrots as well," she continued. "Leave the dirty plate in the sink."

I opened my mouth to ask what the plan was, but Miss Van Lew disappeared up the stairs. "I have things to take care of before *company* comes," she said.

Not long after, Miss Van Lew reappeared and assigned me one of the strangest chores I'd ever heard. But without asking why, I went out the back door and put on the pair of men's boots on the porch. They were just like the ones Miss Van Lew had given to Abraham after he'd delivered the message.

Then I walked around in the muddiest areas of the property and came back. I took the boots off and left them where I'd found them.

"Is it all done?" Miss Van Lew asked when I came back to the kitchen.

"Yes, ma'am," I said. I considered asking Miss Van Lew about the one dirty dish and the boots, but she interrupted my thoughts.

"Charlotte, you are to go outside and watch for company," she said. "Just like you do when Mister McNiven comes. If a wagon approaches, you come get me."

Miss Van Lew went out to the barn where her horse was kept, and I waited on the porch. The only person who approached was Miss Van Lew, leading her horse.

"Hold the door open," she said.

At first I didn't understand what she meant. But then she clucked her tongue and led her horse right on up the steps.

I grabbed the door just in time for Miss Van Lew to enter. But the horse stopped short at the doorway. Her eyes were big and the whites were showing. She looked as confused as I felt.

Miss Van Lew clucked again and said, "Come on now, Ellie."

Ellie lowered her head and let herself be pulled into the living room. I suspected Ellie trusted Miss Van Lew, just like I did. I'd watched Miss Van Lew with her horse. She loved Ellie like she might have loved her own child. That horse loved her right back.

I jumped when Miss Van Lew snapped at me. "Shut the door, Charlotte! Someone might see us."

I closed the door and locked both locks, then stood beside the horse to see what would happen next.

"Go get the carrots," Miss Van Lew said. "Then lure Ellie upstairs."

I almost laughed but realized just in time that Miss Van Lew was serious. I got the carrots while she got Ellie up the stairs and into the very same room I'd been in when I learned the truth about Miss Van Lew, Mister McNiven, and Mary. We left the carrots with Ellie and went back to the kitchen.

Before we could sit down, there was a hard knock at the front door. Miss Van Lew looked at me and said, "Don't forget—slave. Not employee. They cannot know you have any status at all or they will question you."

I nodded and answered the door. I recognized the guard from the prison right away. A big man with a red beard stood next to him. They appeared to be in their twenties, not much older than Mary.

"We're here to see Miss Van Lew," the guard demanded.

I nodded and kept my head down as I led them to the kitchen.

"Robert, what a surprise," Miss Van Lew said when the men walked in behind me. "I was just about to have my supper. You two can join me if you'd like."

"No, thank you," said Robert. "The soldiers need horses. I'm here for yours."

"I don't have a horse anymore," said Miss Van Lew. She looked so sad I almost believed her myself. "I had to sell it. I needed the money."

Robert looked as if he didn't believe a word Miss Van Lew was saying. He turned to the big man with him and said, "Wilson, go outside and search the property."

Once Wilson was gone, Miss Van Lew told me to wash the plate, and I finally understood why. She didn't want to be left alone with these men.

If I was Miss Van Lew, I might have said something smart-mouthed to him, but she sat with him and made small talk about the weather. Just when I put the plate away, Wilson let himself back in the house.

"There's no horse out there," he said. "We might as well leave."

Robert frowned and stood up, and Miss Van Lew said, "Our guests won't be eating here after all, Charlotte. Go to your quarters now." Her voice was steady, but there was the slightest hint of relief in her eyes.

I almost always did what Miss Van Lew said, but I wasn't leaving her alone until I knew they were gone. I went out the back door, grabbed the broom—just in case—and hid in the bushes on the side of the house. If those men tried to hurt her, they'd have another thing coming.

A few minutes later, the door closed and I heard feet on the stairs. But the men didn't leave.

"That woman may have this town fooled, but she's not fooling me," said Robert.

Wilson laughed. "She's just losing her mind. The people in town call her Crazy Bet. She's always wearing old dresses and muttering to herself."

"I don't believe that act for a minute," Robert insisted. "She's always down at Libby, giving presents to the Union soldiers. Everyone knows she favors the coloreds."

No, I thought. *She treats us like human beings.* There was a long silence after that. I held my breath so they wouldn't hear me. Just when I thought I was about to pass out, Robert spoke again:

"I don't care if people think Elizabeth Van Lew is crazy. She's a spy. I'm going to prove it too. Then she'll get what she deserves."

In my eyes, Miss Van Lew deserved a medal for helping other people, but I knew good and well that's not what Robert meant. I had to get inside and warn Miss Van Lew.

CHAPTER FIVE

Richmond, Virginia
Miss Van Lew's home
January 30, 1864

By the time I came out of the bushes, I had cramps in my legs. I went inside through the back door so Miss Van Lew would know it was me. She was still sitting at the kitchen table.

"Bring me those boots, Charlotte," she said when I entered. She sounded mighty calm for a spy who'd just had a visit from the enemy.

"Miss Van Lew, I have to tell you something," I said.

Miss Van Lew's back was to me, and she didn't respond. She had paper in front of her, and at first I thought she was writing a letter. But when I stepped closer, I realized that instead of ink, she was writing with water. There were no words on the paper at all.

I remembered what the men had called her: Crazy Bet.

She's not crazy, I thought to myself, *but she's definitely odd.*

"Charlotte, the boots, please," she repeated.

When I came back with the boots, I blurted out: "Miss Van Lew, Robert knows you're a spy."

Miss Van Lew smiled. "I told you before, Charlotte. I'm not a spy. I'm a patriot. And they won't find anything. They've been here before, snooping around."

"You aren't scared? He said he was going to *prove* it." I watched as she continued to write with the water.

"Charlotte, I have more allies than you can imagine. Slaves, former slaves, abolitionists, prison guards, and men in *both* armies. I'll always know when to expect company," she said.

Miss Van Lew seemed a little too confident. Those men didn't need a reason to hurt her. If they wanted to, they would. I'd seen it more times than I could count on the plantation.

"What are you doing?" I finally asked.

"Sit down and watch," Miss Van Lew told me in reply.

She finished her imaginary writing and picked up another piece of paper. She pretended to write a word on it and set it to the side to dry. Next she popped open the heel of one muddy boot. She folded the first paper, slipped it into the heel of the boot, then replaced it.

"It's a secret message," she explained.

I frowned. It was surely the most secret message anyone had ever received—it was invisible. "How will they read it?" I asked.

Instead of answering, Miss Van Lew poured some milk onto a saucer. Then she dipped the second paper into it. A single word appeared: *Charlotte*.

She looked at me. "There are many ways to send a message, Charlotte. And not one involves getting caught."

———————————————

When I fell asleep in my cabin that night, I dreamed Robert and Wilson came back for Miss Van Lew. I woke up with a start and ran to the house to check on her. She was still sitting at the table. Scraps of paper were scattered in front of her, and one by one she was folding them into the bread dough she had on a pan. I had a feeling this was another one of her "many ways to send a message."

I wasn't exactly sure what to do, so I went outside to wait for Mister McNiven, as usual. It seemed as if the best way to not get caught *being* a spy was to not act like one.

From the front porch, I could see a wagon approaching. I noticed right away that the horse pulling it was darker than Mister McNiven's horse. I hoped it wasn't more "company." A few minutes later, it rolled to a stop in front of me, and Abraham hopped down.

"Good morning," he said. I smiled and led him inside.

When Miss Van Lew saw who was with me, she said, "Let's give our friend a cup of hot coffee."

Abraham sat right down and took off his boots while I poured his coffee.

He seems a little too comfortable, I thought.

But as I watched, Abraham popped open the heel and handed Miss Van Lew a piece of paper. A secret message!

She unfolded it and started reading. First she frowned, then she smiled, and then, suddenly, she stood up. "Charlotte, we have work to do," she said.

Before I could ask what was wrong, Mister McNiven hollered from the front door: "Where is my official greeter today?" The door opened and shut, and soon he stood in the doorway to the kitchen. "There she is! Mornin', Charlotte. It's a good day to be alive."

"Mornin', Mister McNiven," I replied.

Mister McNiven's eyes searched each of our faces, then looked at the unbaked bread on the table.

"Thank you, Abraham," Miss Van Lew said. She gave him the boots with the new message.

Abraham nodded and left without asking about the message in his boot.

Miss Van Lew said, "I think we'd better all have a seat."

The three of us sat at the table together. Mister McNiven handed me a warm loaf, and I broke off pieces of bread for myself and Miss Van Lew.

She took a bite and closed her eyes. "Best bread in Virginia," she said.

Mister McNiven and I waited for Miss Van Lew to finish chewing. Finally she said, "I've received word that there will be a prison break soon. At Libby Prison."

I completely forgot my manners. "The Union soldiers are breaking out?" I asked. I clapped my hands. Not only would they get out of that horrible place, they would be able to join the fight again once they were strong enough.

"There are preparations to be made," Miss Van Lew said. "Thomas, I'll need you to help me stock the house with food. Each day when you bring the bread, I'll need you to bring pork and milk."

Mister McNiven nodded, and Miss Van Lew continued. "I'll get the rooms ready. Charlotte, I have extra blankets and firewood in the barn. You'll need to bring all of that into the house."

"The soldiers will be staying here?" I asked.

Miss Van Lew looked surprised. "Well, of course. We'll hide as many as we can. I've done it before."

My heart tried to leap right out of my chest. *So that's why I saw Union soldiers that night,* I realized. And now *I'd* be able to help the men who were trying to help my people! I'd be doing my part for freedom and justice. This was the most important thing I'd ever done in my life.

Eventually Mister McNiven left, and Miss Van Lew and I busied ourselves preparing for our guests. I wanted to bring the supplies upstairs, but Miss Van Lew said there were rooms I still wasn't allowed to see.

"Leave it at the foot of the stairs," she said. "It's for everyone's safety. If they ask what you know, you won't know everything. No one can know everything."

Once I finished my work, Miss Van Lew gave me outdoor chores, which I usually didn't do. She wanted yard work done, laundry hung, and wood chopped.

"What you'll really be doing," she said, "is keeping watch. If you see anyone at all, you are to let me know as soon as possible—without being seen."

I went out to the edge of the property, where I could see the road below. For a while, no one passed by. But then, just before lunch, a wagon carrying two men went past. One of them was big with a red beard. I was positive I knew who the other man was. Robert and Wilson were up to no good.

I paid attention to every detail: what they were wearing, the markings of the horses, the direction they went when they turned off the road. As soon as the men were out of sight, I carried a stack of wood up to the porch and let Miss Van Lew know.

"Thank you, Charlotte," she said. "I want you to move to another part of the yard now. We don't want it to look as if you're watching the road. But keep your eye on it."

I stayed outside until dark, doing jobs that let me see different parts of the road. Robert and Wilson passed by Church Hill five more times before I went inside. There was no way that was a coincidence. And there was no way we were sneaking Union soldiers into the house with those two circling.

CHAPTER SIX

For a solid week I worked outside in freezing temperatures and kept watch over Miss Van Lew's property. Every day Mister McNiven arrived earlier than usual with more food than usual. I took my loaf of bread and worked at the edges of Miss Van Lew's land. And every day, just before lunch, Robert and Wilson passed by.

Each time I told Miss Van Lew, she said, "That only proves they don't know anything."

The two men traveled the road several times a day, never stopping, but always watching. I had turned into a spy who was spying on men who were spying on us because we were spies. If their trips past the house weren't making me so uneasy, I might have found it funny.

Then, after ten days of waiting, it happened. There was a light tap at the back door just before midnight. Miss Van Lew opened the door to find four escaped prisoners standing there. They were dirty, and their clothes hung from their thin bodies. Even though they looked exhausted, triumph danced in their eyes.

Miss Van Lew ushered them in and led them upstairs. Before she could get them settled in, two more arrived. I let them in. For at least three hours it went on like that—me letting the prisoners in and Miss Van Lew hiding them upstairs. When it was all said and done, we had thirty-two men in the house.

"We must act as if everything is normal," Miss Van Lew said.

If I hadn't seen the soldiers with my own eyes,
I wouldn't have believed they were in the house.
They never made a sound and never came out.
I had no idea which closed doors hid them. Miss
Van Lew gave them food, medicine, clean clothes,
and blankets. She must have had fires going in the
rooms too, because she kept asking for more wood.

Two days after the soldiers arrived, snow fell.
Mister McNiven brought word from Mary, who'd
overheard that some of the escapees had run in
other directions. No one knew what had become
of them, but we were determined that our fugitives
would remain safe.

Each day, I kept watch. Each night, one of
Miss Van Lew's allies would arrive to take soldiers
to safe places, usually to a Union camp or to the
North.

One day, Miss Van Lew called me into the
kitchen. "Charlotte," she said. "I have an important

job for you. I need to start sending you into town
with messages."

"Me?" I said. I wasn't sure I wanted to go
anywhere alone, especially with Robert and Wilson
lurking.

"I can't leave the house unattended," Miss Van
Lew explained. "We're already being watched,
and I'm harboring fugitives. If I leave, we'll most
certainly have unwanted guests."

I knew she was right. The men watching us
were probably just waiting for the right time to go
through the house and look for proof.

"Tomorrow will be your first trip. You'll ride
down the hill with Abraham," Miss Van Lew told
me. "The messages will be passed from you to
former slaves of my father to General Butler or one
of his men. And, Charlotte . . . these messages *must*
be delivered."

The next day I woke up with my stomach in
knots. I didn't know if I was more worried about
getting caught or failing Miss Van Lew. As I sat
next to Abraham in the wagon, I repeated her
instructions in my head.

*Stand in front of the General Store holding
the basket. A woman will smile at you. If she has
a chipped tooth, say hello. If she says, "How is
Babcock?" give her the bread and walk away.*

My legs shook as I made my way to the front
of the store. Miss Van Lew had given me a note to
show anyone who questioned me. It said: *Charlotte
is my servant and is picking up items from the store
for me. —E. Van Lew.*

Without this pass, she'd said, someone might
take me for a runaway slave and capture me. The

thought terrified me, and now the note was a moist ball in my clenched fist.

All I knew about the person I was meeting was that her tooth was chipped, so I squinted at the mouth of every woman who passed. A white woman frowned at me and mumbled. A young colored woman smiled at me, but her tooth wasn't chipped.

Just when I started to wonder if something had gone wrong, a woman with a chipped tooth smiled at me. We had our little conversation, I handed her the bread, and she hurried down the sidewalk. I hurried off in the other direction.

Miss Van Lew sent me to town with a different basket each time. One day it was a dozen eggs that looked normal, except that three or four were hollowed out with a message inside. Another day it was a message baked into a loaf of bread. Sometimes it was a book with a coded message inside.

By day, I snuck through town, delivering messages. By night, I crouched in Miss Van Lew's bushes, keeping watch as allies arrived to lead our hidden soldiers, a few at a time, to the North. I treated every job as if my life depended on it— because it did.

After the first few trips into town, my nerves settled. Abraham and I began to talk all the way there and all the way back.

"Abraham, were you one of Miss Van Lew's daddy's slaves?" I asked one day.

Abraham nodded. "Indeed I was." Then he laughed. "She used to argue with her daddy all the time. Trying to get him to free all of us."

"She fought with her own daddy?" I asked.

Abraham looked at me. "Sure did," he said. "That woman is something else. A lot of people don't like her, but they leave her—and all of us— alone. The Van Lew name carries a lot of power."

"Were you a slave at the same time as Mary?"
I asked.

Abraham nodded. "I was. I bet you miss seeing her every day."

I sighed. "I sure do."

Between the errands and keeping watch, Miss Van Lew kept me busy. Mister McNiven was busy too. He barely came inside when he delivered the bread in the mornings. But even though he was rushing, he still found time to say, "Mornin', Charlotte. It's a good day to be alive."

Now that I was a spy too, I finally understood why Mister McNiven always said that. He knew he was doing something important. He hoped for a better tomorrow and was trying to do his part.

One day when Mister McNiven greeted me, I replied, "A good day, indeed."

He chuckled when I said that, and I smiled while I watched his wagon disappear down the hill.

Most of our Union soldiers had gone, but we still had a few left, so we remained watchful. When there was time, Miss Van Lew and I removed any evidence that the men had stayed with us. She carried supplies from the secret rooms down the stairs, and I hid them back in the barn.

One day Miss Van Lew said, "I need your help with something, Charlotte."

I was always happy to help Miss Van Lew. *I wonder if she'll finally let me into one of the secret rooms to clean it,* I thought.

"I need you to deliver a book to Charles at Libby Prison," she said.

That was the last thing I had expected Miss Van Lew to say, and it was the *very* last thing I wanted to do. I was nervous enough delivering messages in town. I'd be scared to death at Libby by myself. From what I'd seen, there were few places more depressing, or dirty, or hateful, or dangerous than Libby Prison.

Miss Van Lew must have seen the fear on my face. "I have a friend in Libby Prison—Erasmus Ross," she told me. "He's a Confederate guard. You'll recognize him by the scar that runs from his cheek to his ear. If something goes wrong, try to find him."

A burning feeling started in my stomach, and it rose until it was in my throat. I tried to ignore it. If Miss Van Lew was willing to sacrifice her money, reputation, and life to help free my people, then I'd sacrifice all I had to do the same.

I focused on my breathing so Miss Van Lew wouldn't hear the panic in my voice and forced myself to look her right in her eyes. "Yes, ma'am."

CHAPTER SEVEN

The next day I stood outside of Libby Prison, far enough away so that I wouldn't draw anyone's attention. I wasn't ready to go in. My ride down the hill with Abraham had been silent, and when he'd dropped me off several buildings away, he had said his only words: "Good luck, Charlotte."

I'd hoped the short walk to Libby would help me calm down, but it only gave me time to imagine all the things that could go wrong. One of Miss Van Lew's messages could get discovered. One of the Confederate men could decide to give me a hard time. But my worst fear was that Robert and Wilson would discover the message and kill me.

I went over all the tips Miss Van Lew had given me before I left. *Head down. Eyes down. Speak only if spoken to. Get the book to Charles first. Halt the mission if needed.*

I forced myself to put one foot in front of the other. As I approached the prison, a guard came to meet me. I was relieved to see it was the same one from my first visit with Miss Van Lew. I looked down and waited until he spoke.

"What's your business here, little girl?" he asked.

"I have a delivery from Miss Van Lew, sir," I answered.

I didn't dare look at his face, but he was quiet for some time. Finally he said, "I'll be happy to take it off your hands."

I knew the prisoners would never see any of it if I let him do that. "Sir, Miss Van Lew ordered me to hand deliver these gifts to the soldiers," I explained. "She wants me to apologize to them for not coming herself."

The guard made a snorting sound. "Where is she anyway?"

I repeated exactly what I'd been told to say. "She's taken quite ill, sir. But she got out of bed to make you this." I handed him a chunk of gingerbread and a bottle of buttermilk.

The guard took it greedily. *Miss Van Lew was right*, I thought. *He is easy to please.*

"All right, then. Make it fast," he said.

I hurried along before the guard could change his mind. There were more guards than had been there the first time, so I stayed close to the wall of the prison. The last thing I wanted was to be surrounded.

I kept my head down and walked in. At the foot
of the stairs I heard a familiar voice.

"Well, look who we have here," said Robert.

There was a laugh and another voice said,
"Miss Van Lew's little pet."

Robert pulled one of my braids, and I bit my
bottom lip. Several men laughed. I had to get away
from them . . . quick. I was about to offer him the
extra bread in the basket, but a shout came from the
top of the stairs.

"Y'all move out of the way!"

Two men in Confederate uniforms came down
the stairs carrying a dead Union soldier. They tried
to cover him, but I caught a glimpse of his face.
I could tell he had been beaten.

As soon as they went by, I ran up the stairs
to the second floor. There was only one guard in
the room. I spotted Charles and went directly to
him. Miss Van Lew had told me to get his book

to him right away, in case things took a turn for the worse.

"I remember you," said Charles.

I kept my head down and handed him the book. "Here, sir. From Miss Van Lew."

"What's your name?" asked Charles.

I raised my head a bit and saw dark circles under both his eyes. He was so thin his cheekbones stuck out. He didn't look as if he had the strength to read a book.

I whispered so no one would hear me. "Charlotte, sir."

Charles handed me a book to return to Miss Van Lew. Then he leaned forward and whispered, "You're a brave girl, Charlotte, but you've picked the wrong day to come. Make your deliveries and get out of here."

I don't know how, but I knew Charles was telling the truth. I nodded and started handing out boiled eggs and bread to the other soldiers. One lay on the wooden floor with no covers. He shivered and whimpered. I was pretty sure he had a fever. I bent down to put bread near him and saw that his hair was alive with lice.

Three rats came out of the wall and nibbled at the bread. I backed away and tripped over two prisoners playing chess on the floor. The game pieces scattered, and I waited for them to shout at me.

"This is no place for you," one of the men said. "These guards will eat you alive."

As soon as the words were out of his mouth, a hush fell over the room. I turned and saw Robert and Wilson blocking the door. They both had smirks on their faces. Charles stood up and slowly walked toward me.

Robert pulled out a gun and pointed it right at me. "Get over here, girl," he said.

My feet were heavier than bricks and were glued to the floor. They wouldn't move. All eyes were on the doorway.

Robert growled at me. "I said get over here. *Now,*" he demanded. He walked toward me, put the barrel of his gun in my face, and cocked it.

Charles lunged forward, but he was no match for the two Confederates. He was too skinny and weak. Wilson shoved him out of the way and laughed.

"Today you're gon' tell me all of Miss Van Lew's little secrets," said Robert.

Just then a third man in a Confederate uniform arrived. "What's going on in here?" he demanded.

Robert laughed again. "We caught us a little colored spy."

The new guard was in front of me in three long strides. I put my head down, but he grabbed my chin, squeezed my cheeks, and forced my face up.

I closed my eyes. I could feel his hot breath in my face.

"Look at me," the guard said.

He squeezed even harder, and a sharp pain shot through my jaw. I was afraid to open my eyes, but I was even more afraid not to.

CHAPTER EIGHT

Richmond, Virginia
Libby Prison
February 19, 1864

I opened my eyes. The man had a scar from his cheek to his ear. It had to be Erasmus Ross, the man Miss Van Lew had told me about, but there was no way he was her actual friend.

"I know just what to do with your kind," Mister Ross said. He grabbed Miss Van Lew's basket and shoved me to the door.

"You're gonna get it now," said Wilson. He and Robert laughed.

Mister Ross pushed me along in front of him. We went down the stairs, out the door, and around the back of Libby Prison. When we got to a spot where nobody could hear, he finally stopped.

"I'm going to get you out of here," he whispered, "but I have to hit you. I want you to scream like it hurts."

Relief rushed through me. He *was* a friend. I took a deep breath and braced myself.

Mister Ross tossed the basket, grabbed my shoulders, and shook me. "Don't you know better than to meddle in Confederate business?" he hollered.

I cried. "I'm sorry. Please don't hurt me," I begged.

"You ain't sorry enough!" he yelled. He drew his hand up and across his body.

The backhand came at me quickly. It hurt, but not nearly as much as it should have. I screamed and carried on. Mister Ross gave me a shove so hard it sent me to my knees.

"Get out of here and don't come back!" he yelled.

I picked up Miss Van Lew's basket and ran away from Libby Prison as fast as I could. I could barely see through the tears in my eyes. I was crying, partly because my face hurt and partly because I was relieved to get away.

A moment later, a shot rang out behind me. I could only hope that Mister Ross had fired into the air.

I ran to the street where Abraham was waiting in the wagon. He took one look at me and jumped down. He took the basket from my trembling hands and put it in the wagon. Then he picked me up and hugged me tight.

"It's OK. It's over now," he whispered over and over again.

I cried into Abraham's shoulder, and he rocked from side to side until I stopped.

Miss Van Lew was sitting in a rocking chair on the porch when we got back to Church Hill. She was wrapped in a blanket, but when she saw my face she bolted right out of that chair. "What have those fools done to you?" she demanded.

She took a close look at my face where I'd been slapped. *Mister Ross must have left a mark,* I thought.

Miss Van Lew led me inside and made me hot tea with extra honey in it. She made me some eggs, ham, and buttered toast too. Then she, Abraham, and I sat at the kitchen table while I ate every last crumb on my plate. Abraham shook his head, and Miss Van Lew muttered words like *unbelievable* as I told them what had happened at Libby Prison.

When I was done talking, Miss Van Lew pounded both fists on the table and cursed.

"They make me sick," she said. "Bothering little girls. Killing innocent men."

"It was just the one dead man at Libby, Miss Van Lew," I said.

Miss Van Lew let out the saddest sigh I'd ever heard. "No, Charlotte. *Men.* I received word today that they recaptured forty-eight Union soldiers. Men who didn't stay with us. Two of them drowned, and it's all because of the Confederates."

My eyes filled with tears again. Going back to Libby Prison must have been horrible. I imagined having to go back to the plantation where I'd once lived, and I suddenly felt very tired.

"I'm sorry I caused a ruckus at Libby Prison, Miss Van Lew," I said.

Miss Van Lew shook her head. "That was no mission for a child, but you were the only one who could get in. They're suspicious of everybody right now. But you delivered the message. You succeeded."

I realized she was right. Despite all that had gone wrong, the message had been delivered.

"What did the message say?" I asked.

Miss Van Lew shook her head once again. "Remember what I told you, Charlotte," she said. "No one can know everything."

I was quiet for a moment. My muscles ached, and after the day I'd had, all I wanted was to lie down. I missed Mary. We used to eat together in our cabin, and she'd tell me stories of her time in the North until I fell asleep.

But now she was gone, and for the first time, I felt like I really needed her.

"Miss Van Lew, can I go see Mary tomorrow?" I asked.

"No," said Miss Van Lew. "It's too risky."

The answer didn't surprise me, but I was sad anyway. I said good night and made my way to my cabin. It was the best place I'd ever lived. It had real windows, a wooden floor, a little table, and two chairs. It also had a cot for me to sleep on. There was a second cot for Mary.

When she'd left, I'd made up her cot nice and neat for her. I hadn't touched it since. Tonight, though, after I lit a fire and wrapped up in a blanket, I lay down on Mary's cot. I kept my eyes on the fire, because every time I closed them I saw the barrel of a gun pointed at my head.

All night long, wild thoughts crept in and out of my mind. I saw Robert and his red-bearded friend. I saw Erasmus Ross. I saw the dead prisoner and the rats and the lice. And when that got to be too much, I imagined Mary's face.

I wondered what Miss Van Lew would do if I decided to see Mary anyway. It might be dangerous, but I was no longer a slave. I was free. And Miss Van Lew had brought me here to be with family.

I'd learned a lot about being sneaky from Miss Van Lew. Maybe I'd just sneak on over to the Confederate White House during my next errand. Miss Van Lew would never even know it.

By the time the fire died I'd made up my mind. Whether Miss Van Lew liked it or not, I was going to see my cousin. And I wasn't going to get caught.

CHAPTER NINE

Richmond, Virginia
February 26, 1864

I had to wait a full week before I got the perfect chance to sneak away to see Mary. The fugitives had all gone, but now Miss Van Lew really *had* fallen ill. She had a cough that had settled deep in her chest.

She wanted me to make a delivery, but it had to be done very early in the morning. She'd been more cautious after my trip to Libby and thought it best for me to finish before breakfast.

"Charlotte, ride down the hill with Abraham and deliver this," Miss Van Lew said, placing a basket of eggs on the table. "There will be a colored gentleman with boots like Abraham's waiting on the corner. His right boot lace will be untied. Abraham will have more to do in town, so you'll need to wait for him at the bottom of the hill. Stay hidden."

That's perfect, I thought. *I can go see Mary while I wait.*

I picked up the small basket. I didn't have to shake the eggs to know that some of them contained pieces of a message. I no longer asked what they said. After my close call at Libby, I understood why it was safer not to know.

Abraham let me off in the middle of town and went on his way. I walked until I found the man Miss Van Lew had described.

"Mighty fine morning," I said, just like I was supposed to—even though the morning was so cold the street was empty.

"I sure do miss Babcock," the man replied.

That was my signal. I handed the man the eggs and then headed off on my own mission—to see Mary.

Abraham had pointed out the Confederate White House during one of our earlier trips to town. He'd told me all about it. President Davis lived there and had all the Confederate Army meetings there too. Abraham and I didn't think of him as the president. We already had a real president—President Lincoln.

Halfway to the Confederate White House, my nerves started to get to me. Miss Van Lew would be furious if she found out what I was doing. She might not let me work for her anymore—not spy work or any other kind, for that matter.

I realized Mary might be mad at me too. I could get her in trouble, just by showing up.

I stopped on the side of the road in front of the White House and stared at it. It was three stories tall, and of course, it was all white. It was so early that all the curtains were still drawn. The house looked like it was asleep, and I prayed it wouldn't wake up. That would be the end of me and my missions.

Just as I was about to turn around and leave, the door opened. Mary came out, carrying a basket of laundry. She walked toward a clothesline on the side of the house.

I couldn't believe it. It was like I was meant to see her. I couldn't leave now. As I inched closer, I kept checking to make sure no one was in sight.

"Please don't get caught; please don't get caught," I whispered to myself.

Before I could approach Mary, she noticed me. Her jaw dropped, and she glanced around. Then she quickly hung a large bedsheet.

Even though I wanted to hug my cousin tight and not let go, I snuck over and squatted behind it. It was too dangerous to do anything else.

"Charlotte!" Mary said. It was a whisper and a yell at the same time. "What are you doing here?"

"I miss you, cousin. I couldn't stand it anymore," I whispered back.

Mary peeked around the sheet and smiled at me. "I miss you too," she said. "Are you all right? How did you get here?"

"I work for Miss Van Lew now," I said.

Mary giggled. "I know. I was there when she bought your freedom, remember?"

"No," I said. "I mean I *work* for Miss Van Lew."

Mary's eyes nearly jumped out of her head. "You do? Mister McNiven didn't tell me."

I said to Mary what Miss Van Lew had said to me: "No one can know everything."

Just then a woman's voice shouted from the White House porch. I couldn't see her, but I heard her loud and clear. "Mary, hurry up! We're hungry!"

"That woman never gives me a minute's rest," Mary muttered. "She's about to make me miss my chance to talk to Mister McNiven."

"Mary!" shouted the woman again.

"Yes, Missus Davis," said Mary. She hung up the pants she had in her hands. "I'll be right along."

I heard a wagon approaching. Mary and I turned to see Mister McNiven coming down the road for his daily bread delivery.

"Are you giving him a message today?" I asked.

"I can't," said Mary. "I won't have time. But *you* will."

I hoped my memory was as good as Mary's. I nodded and got my mind ready to take in every word Mary said.

"Tell Mister McNiven I heard Mister Davis talking to the general last night over dinner," Mary said. "They're moving an installment of prisoners on Monday, February twenty-ninth."

The date was easy to remember, but I repeated the word *installment* a few times in my head. I didn't know what that meant.

"They're moving four hundred men south, to Georgia," Mary continued. "Another installment will be moved on March second. Can you remember all that?"

"Yes," I whispered. I *had* to remember.

"Good," said Mary. "I love you, Charlotte." And then she was gone.

I peeked from behind the sheet as Mary ran toward the house. Mister McNiven stopped the wagon and climbed down. Missus Davis hollered for Mary again, and Mister McNiven turned around and spotted me. Worry spread all over his face as he looked from me to Mary to the woman on the porch I couldn't see.

As Mary passed by, Mister McNiven handed her the bread. She took it without even stopping to speak. I heard the door slam, and Mister McNiven motioned for me to come to his wagon.

I felt like my legs had frozen solid while I squatted behind the bedsheet. They wouldn't move. If I ran out, there were at least a hundred things that might go wrong. Missus Davis might open the door to say something to Mister McNiven. She could open the curtains. She'd be able to see the wagon from the window.

There was nowhere to go. I was trapped at the Confederate White House.

CHAPTER TEN

Mister McNiven frowned and motioned again. I couldn't stay there forever. And the later it got, the worse off I'd be. Fear got my blood pumping through my veins and down to my legs, and I ran to the wagon.

As soon as Mister McNiven saw me coming, he jumped in. I jumped in right after him. He smacked his horse with the reins, and the wagon jerked forward.

We rode in silence for a long while. Finally Mister McNiven said, "What were you thinking?

You compromised us all." I could hear the disappointment in his voice.

I knew he was right, but I also knew I had done something important. Without me, Mary's message would have had to wait for another day. By then it might have been too late.

"I have a message from Mary," I said.

Mister McNiven stopped watching the road and stared at me. "What kind of message?" he asked.

I smiled and said, "A secret message. She asked me to tell it to you."

"Don't tell it to me," said Mister McNiven. "Save it for Miss Elizabeth."

A wagon headed toward us, and we stopped talking. It was Abraham, and when he saw me riding with Mister McNiven he halted his wagon. Abraham looked confused, but when Mister McNiven told him we were headed back to Church Hill, he nodded and went on his way.

"Mister McNiven, do you think Miss Van Lew will be mad at me?" I asked.

He thought for a while. "Yes, I think so. But if your message is important, she'll forgive you," he said.

Mister McNiven and I found Miss Van Lew sitting in the library. She wore a shawl around her shoulders and steam rose from a cup of tea on the table. She didn't look surprised to see us together, probably because this was about the time Mister McNiven usually delivered the bread.

"Good morning, Thomas," she said. Then she looked at me. "Did you make your delivery, Charlotte?"

"Yes, ma'am," I said. I didn't know how to tell her what else I had done.

Mister McNiven did, though. "That's not all she did," he said. "I found her with Mary at the Confederate White House."

Miss Van Lew leaned forward in her chair.

"Charlotte, I *told* you not to go over there," she said.

"I know, but I needed to see my cousin," I said. I hoped Miss Van Lew would understand. After all, she was the one who brought us together in the first place.

She said, "You put us all at risk."

Mister McNiven interrupted again. "She has a message for you from Mary," he said. "I got there too late for Mary to tell me."

A clock on the shelf ticked while I waited for her to answer. Finally she leaned back and said, "Well, Charlotte, what is it?"

I stood up straight and repeated word for word what Mary had told me. I didn't forget a single word. Not even *installment*.

I could tell the message was important, because Mister McNiven smiled and winked at me, and Miss Van Lew's eyes got big. When I was done, she said,

"We need to notify General Butler immediately. This can't wait until tomorrow."

Mister McNiven got a serious expression on his face, and he left without a word. As soon as he was gone, Miss Van Lew said, "Sit down, Charlotte."

I sat on the edge of a chair near Miss Van Lew and waited for my punishment.

"You never should have gone over there," she said. "You're lucky you didn't give us away—or worse."

I lowered my eyes. "Yes, ma'am."

Miss Van Lew stared at me for a long time. "But . . . ," she finally said. "This message could help free four hundred Union prisoners. It could give the Union a chance to attack."

I nodded. "I hope so."

"Even though things worked out in our favor, you defied me," she said. "Don't let that happen again."

"No, ma'am. I won't," I promised.

"Thank you, Charlotte," she said. "I'm glad to have you on our side."

When she said that, I knew that I was forgiven. "Do you think we'll win the war?" I asked.

Miss Van Lew sighed and sipped her tea. "We have to believe we will," she said. "We have to try."

I nodded. Miss Van Lew was right. I had to try. I'd succeeded at each mission so far, including Libby Prison. I'd just have to continue to survive, one mission at a time. As long as we fought for what was right, there was still hope.

I stood up to leave Miss Van Lew to her tea and her book. But when I reached the door, I turned back and smiled. "It's a good day to be alive," I said.

A NOTE FROM THE AUTHOR

At first, I wasn't sure how to approach the topic of the Civil War. I didn't want the story to be violent, or too sad, or . . . boring. During the four-year war, which lasted from 1861–1865, Americans in the North (known as the Union) fought against Americans in the South (known as the Confederates). Southerners supported slavery, and Northerners did not. Southern states even seceded (withdrew) from the United States. Many battles were fought. I needed to narrow down a broad topic—and I had some serious research to do.

As soon as I learned about Elizabeth Van Lew and her spy ring, the Richmond Union Underground, I knew what my book would be about: a spy ring run by a woman—and my main character would be a girl who joined them in the fight for justice. I would include many real people and events.

The following people in my story were real: Elizabeth Van Lew, Mary (full name: Mary Elizabeth Bowser), Thomas McNiven, President Davis and his wife, President Lincoln, General Butler, and Erasmus

Ross—minus the fictional scar. I kept these people in their real roles during the war. Elizabeth Van Lew's background, the locations, and the Libby Prison break were also real.

People who were part of the spy ring went on missions much like Charlotte's. However, Charlotte and her missions are fictional. I had to make up a lot of the details, because . . . well . . . spies keep secrets. No one really knows the details of the Richmond Union Underground. Elizabeth Van Lew kept a journal, which was buried in her yard. Only half of the journal was found, and it was destroyed at her direction. After the war, Miss Van Lew asked that all her spy materials be returned to her by General Butler. He agreed, and she destroyed them all.

Elizabeth Van Lew is recognized as a key source of information to the Union during the Civil War. She used invisible ink, loaves of bread, brogans (boots) with false heels, and hollowed-out eggs to deliver messages. She also hid messages in books by underlining words and punching small holes. Eventually she used a "cipher code" to write out the messages. A copy of that code was found folded in the back of her watch when she died.

Elizabeth Van Lew's house was large enough to hide Union soldiers until they could be taken to safety. It was full of secret passages and rooms, just like the homes used in the Underground Railroad. (One source says the Van Lew Estate was used as a station on the Underground Railroad before the war.) At one time, Miss Van Lew had more than one hundred Union soldiers hiding in her house—and she really *did* hide her horse in the house to keep the Confederates from taking it!

Unfortunately, some people called Elizabeth Van Lew "Crazy Bet." Perhaps this is because she spent most of her fortune helping African-Americans and the Union. Elizabeth did some odd things on purpose. She knew that if people thought she was "crazy," they wouldn't pay attention to what she was *really* doing. She wore tattered clothes and strange hats and walked through town swinging a basket. She muttered to herself and sang silly songs. Nevertheless, Elizabeth Van Lew was one of the most intelligent and cunning

Elizabeth Van Lew (October 12, 1818–September 25, 1900) spent her life in Richmond, Virginia, where she worked as one of the Union's most important spies during the Civil War.

people of her time. She considered herself a patriot, not a spy. In her journal she wrote:

A person cannot be called a spy for serving their country within its recognized borders. Am I now to be branded a spy by my own country for which I was willing to lay down my life . . .

Mary Elizabeth Bowser was as important to the Richmond Union Underground as Elizabeth Van Lew. Her background in this story is true. Mary was very smart and had a photographic memory. She could also read, which was very unusual for African-Americans at that time—especially those who were enslaved. Mary worked in the Confederate White House and sent Confederate secrets, plans, and strategies to Elizabeth Van Lew. She too was underestimated, both as a woman and an African-American.

After the Civil War ended, Mary practically disappeared. She changed her name and there is little information available about her. Photos reported to be Mary Elizabeth Bowser may not actually be of her. In 1995, Mary Elizabeth Bowser was inducted into the U.S. Army Military Intelligence Corps Hall of Fame.

History was never my favorite subject in school. It wasn't until I was a teenager and started learning about the history that *wasn't* in my textbooks that I began to find it interesting. If you've ever wondered if people like *you* played an important part in historic events, I can guarantee you they did. Be curious. Be determined. *Spy* on history. Look for the small details, little-known facts, and secrets. History is fascinating, and you'll find many unsung heroes and "sheroes"— some of whom might be just like you.

GLOSSARY

abolitionists (ab-uh-LISH-uh-nists)—people in favor of stopping slavery

allies (AL-ahyz)—people, groups, or nations associated or united with another in a common purpose

cipher (SAHY-fer)—a method of secret writing or the alphabet or letters and symbols used in such writing

coincidence (koh-IN-si-duhns)—a situation in which things happen at the same time without planning

Confederate (Kuhn-FED-er-it)—a soldier of or a person who sided with the Southern Confederacy

harboring (HAHR-ber-ing)—giving shelter to someone

installment (in-STAWL-muhnt)—one of several parts of something presented over a period of time

invaluable (in-VAL-yoo-uh-buhl)—priceless

fugitive (FYOO-ji-tiv)—a person who is running away

meddle (MED-L)—to be overly involved in someone else's business

patriot (PEY-tree-uht)—a person who loves his or her country and strongly supports it

quarters (KWAWR-ters)—lodging or shelter

triumph (TRAHY-uhmf)—to celebrate victory or success in high spirits

MAKING CONNECTIONS

1. In Chapter Two, Miss Van Lew tells Charlotte that Libby Prison will be, "the most horrible place you've ever been." Charlotte doubts this is true, because she's "seen slavery." What do you think Charlotte means by this? Give evidence from the text to support your answer. (You may use information in other chapters to support your answer.)

2. Charlotte has been missing her cousin, Mary, for a long time. Why do you think she chooses the moment she does to finally visit Mary? Give at least three reasons and support them with evidence from the text.

3. At the end of the book, Charlotte repeats what Mister McNiven often says to her: "It's a good day to be alive." Do you agree or disagree with that statement? Why?

ABOUT THE AUTHOR

Nikki Shannon Smith is from Oakland, California, but she now lives in the Central Valley with her husband and two children. She has worked in elementary education for more than twenty-five years and writes everything from picture books to young adult novels. When she's not busy with family, work, or writing, she loves to visit the coast. The first thing she packs in her suitcase is always a book.